The Adventures of Jerry Muskrat

By THORNTON W. BURGESS

Illustrated by HARRISON CADY

PUBLISHERS

Grosset & Dunlap

NEW YORK

BY ARRANGEMENT WITH LITTLE, BROWN & COMPANY

PRINTED IN THE UNITED STATES OF AMERICA

The Adventures of Jerry Muskrat

Contents

[v]

CONTENTS

Illustrations

ILLUSTRATIONS

The Adventures of
Jerry Muskrat

I

Jerry Muskrat
Has a Fright

WHAT was it Mother Muskrat
had said about Farmer
Brown's boy and his traps? Jerry
Muskrat sat on the edge of the
Big Rock and kicked his heels
while he tried to remember.
The fact is, Jerry had not half
heeded. He had been thinking
of other things. Besides, it

seemed to him that Mother Muskrat was altogether foolish about a great many things.

"Pooh!" said Jerry, throwing out his chest, "I guess I can take care of myself without being tied to my mother's apron strings! What if Farmer Brown's boy is setting traps around the Smiling Pool? I guess he can't fool your Uncle Jerry. He isn't so smart as he thinks he is; I can fool him any day." Jerry chuckled. He was thinking of how he had once fooled Farmer Brown's boy into thinking a big trout was on his hook.

Slowly Jerry slid into the Smiling Pool and swam over toward his favorite log.

Peter Rabbit stuck his head over the edge of the bank. "Hi, Jerry," he shouted, "last night I saw Farmer Brown's boy coming over this way with a lot of traps. Better watch out!"

"Go chase yourself, Peter Rabbit. I guess I can look out for myself," replied Jerry, just a little crossly.

Peter made a wry face and started for the sweet clover patch. Hardly was he out of sight when Billy Mink and Bobby Coon came down the Laughing Brook together. They seemed very much excited. When they saw Jerry Muskrat, they beckoned for him to come over where they were, and when he got there, they both talked at once and it was all about Farmer Brown's boy and his traps.

"You'd better watch out, Jerry," warned Billy Mink, who is a great traveler and has had wide experience.

"Oh, I guess I'm able to take care of myself," said Jerry airily, and once more started for his favorite log. And what do you suppose he was thinking about as he swam along? He was wishing that he knew what a trap looked like, for despite his boasting he didn't even know what he was to look out for. As he drew near his favorite log, something tickled his nose. He stopped swimming to sniff and sniff. My, how good it did smell! And it seemed to come right straight from the old log. Jerry began to swim as fast as he could. In a few minutes he scrambled out on the old log. Then Jerry rubbed his eyes three times to be sure that he saw aright. There were luscious pieces of carrot lying right in front of him.

[5]

Now there is nothing that Jerry Muskrat likes better than carrot. So he didn't stop to wonder how it got there. He just reached out for the nearest piece and ate it. Then he reached for the next piece and ate it. Then he did a funny little dance just for joy. When he was quite out of breath, he sat down to rest.

Snap! Something had Jerry Muskrat by the tail! Jerry squealed with fright and pain. Oh, how it did hurt! He twisted and turned, but he was held fast and could not see what had him. Then he pulled and pulled, until it seemed as if his tail would pull off. But it didn't. So he kept pulling, and pretty soon the thing let go so suddenly that Jerry tumbled headfirst into the water.

When he reached home, Mother Muskrat did his sore tail up for him. "What did I tell you about traps?" she asked severely.

Jerry stopped crying. "Was that a trap?" he asked. Then he remembered that in his fright he didn't even see it. "Oh dear," he moaned, "I wouldn't know one today if I met it."

II

The Convention
at the Big Rock

JOLLY, round, red Mr. Sun
looked down on the Smiling
Pool. He almost forgot to keep
on climbing up in the blue sky,
he was so interested in what he
saw there. What do you think
it was? Why, it was a convention at the Big Rock, the
queerest convention he ever had
seen. Your daddy would say that

it was a mass meeting of angry citizens. Maybe it was, but that is a pretty long term. Anyway, Mother Muskrat said it was a convention, and she ought to know, for she is the one who had called it.

Of course Jerry Muskrat was there, and his uncles and aunts and all his cousins. Billy Mink was there, and all his relations, even old Grandfather Mink, who has lost most of his teeth and is a little hard of hearing.

Little Joe Otter was there, with his father and mother and all his relations even to his third cousins. Bobby Coon was there,

*Bobby Coon brought with him every Coon
of his acquaintance*

and he had brought with him every Coon of his acquaintance who ever fished in the Smiling Pool or along the Laughing Brook. And everybody was looking very solemn, very solemn indeed.

When the last one had arrived, Mother Muskrat climbed up on the Big Rock and called Jerry Muskrat up beside her, where all could see him. Then she made a speech. "Friends of the Smiling Pool and Laughing Brook," began Mrs. Muskrat, "I have called you together to show you what has happened to my son Jerry and to ask your advice." She stopped and pointed to Jerry's sore tail. "What do you think did that?" she demanded.

"Probably Jerry's been in a fight and got whipped," said Bobby Coon to his neighbor, for Bobby Coon is a graceless young scamp and does not always show proper respect to his neighbors.

Mrs. Muskrat glared at him, for she had overheard the remark. Then she held up one hand to command silence. "Friends, it was a trap—a trap set by Farmer Brown's boy! A trap to catch you and me and our children!" said she solemnly. "It is no longer safe for our little folks to play around the Smiling Pool or along the Laughing Brook. What are we going to do about it?"

Everybody looked at everybody else in dismay. Then everybody began to talk at once, and if Farmer Brown's boy could have heard all the things said about him, his cheeks certainly would have burned. Indeed, I am afraid that they would have blistered. Such excitement! Everybody had a different idea, and nobody would listen to anybody else. Old Mr. Mink lost his temper and called Grandpa Otter a meddlesome know-nothing. It looked very much as if the convention was going to break up in a sad quarrel. Then Mr. Coon climbed up on the Big Rock and with a stick pounded for silence.

"I move," said he, "that inasmuch as we cannot agree, we tell Great-Grandfather Frog all about the danger and ask his advice, for he is very old and very wise and remembers when the world was young. All in favor please raise their right hands."

At once the air was full of hands, and everybody was good-natured once more. So it was agreed to call in Great-Grandfather Frog.

III

The Oracle of the Smiling Pool

GRANDFATHER FROG sat on his big green lily pad with his eyes half closed, for all the world as if he knew nothing about the meeting at the Big Rock. Of course he did know, for there isn't much going on around the Smiling Pool which he doesn't see or at least hear all about. The Merry Little Breezes, who are here, there, and everywhere, told him all that was going on, so that when he saw Jerry Muskrat and Little Joe Otter swimming toward him, he knew what they were coming for. But he pretended to be very much surprised when Jerry Muskrat very politely said:

"Good morning, Grandfather Frog."

"Good morning, Jerry Muskrat. You're out early this morning," replied Grandfather Frog.

"If you please, you are wanted over at the Big Rock," said Jerry.

Grandfather Frog's eyes twinkled, but he made his voice very deep and gruff as he replied, "Chugarum! You're a scamp, Jerry Muskrat, and Little Joe Otter is another. What trick are you trying to play on me now?"

Jerry Muskrat and Little Joe Otter looked a wee bit sheepish, for it was true that they were forever trying to play tricks on Grandfather Frog.

"Really and truly, Grandfather Frog, there isn't any trick this time," said Jerry. "There is a meeting at the Big Rock to try to decide what to do to keep

Farmer Brown's boy from setting traps around the Smiling Pool and along the Laughing Brook, and everybody wants your advice, because you are so old and so wise. Please come."

Grandfather Frog smoothed down his white and yellow waistcoat and pretended to think the matter over very seriously, while Jerry and Little Joe fidgeted impatiently. Finally he spoke.

"I am very old, as you have said, Jerry Muskrat, and it is a long way over to the Big Rock."

"Get right on my back and I'll take you over there," said Jerry eagerly.

"I'm afraid that you'll spill me off," replied Grandfather Frog.

"No, I won't; just try me and see," begged Jerry.

So Grandfather Frog climbed on Jerry Muskrat's back, and Jerry started for the Big Rock as fast as he could go. When all the Minks and the Otters and the Coons and the Muskrats saw them coming, they gave a great shout, for Grandfather Frog is sometimes called the oracle of the Smiling Pool. You know an oracle is one who is very wise.

Bobby Coon helped Grandfather Frog up on the Big Rock, and when he had made himself comfortable,

Jerry started for the Big Rock as fast as he could go

Mrs. Muskrat told him all about Farmer Brown's boy and his traps, and how Jerry had been caught in one by the tail, and she ended by asking for his advice, because they all knew that he was so wise.

When she said this, Grandfather Frog puffed himself up until it seemed as if his white and yellow waistcoat would surely burst. He sat very still for a while and gazed straight at jolly, round, red Mr. Sun without blinking once. Then he spoke in a very deep voice:

"Tomorrow morning at sunrise I will tell you what to do," said he. And not another word could they get out of him.

IV

Grandfather Frog's Plan

JUST as Old Mother West Wind and her Merry Little Breezes came down from the Purple Hills, and jolly, round, red Mr. Sun threw his nightcap off and began his daily climb up in the blue sky, Great-Grandfather Frog climbed up on the Big Rock in the Smiling Pool. Early as he was, all the little people who live along the Laughing Brook and around the Smiling Pool were waiting for him. Bobby Coon had found two traps set by Farmer Brown's boy, and Billy Mink had almost stepped in a third. No one felt safe any more, yet no one knew what to do. So they all waited for the advice of Great-Grandfather Frog, who, you know, is accounted very, very wise.

Grandfather Frog cleared his throat. "Chugarum!" said he. "You must find all the traps that Farmer Brown's boy has set."

"How are we going to do it?" asked Bobby Coon.

"By looking for them," replied Grandfather Frog tartly.

Bobby Coon looked foolish and slipped out of sight behind his mother.

"All the Coons and all the Minks must search along the banks of the Laughing Brook, and all the Muskrats and all the Otters must search along the banks of the Smiling Pool. You must use your eyes and your noses. When you find things good to eat where you never found them before, watch out! When you get the first whiff of the man-smell, watch out! Billy Mink, you are small and quick, and your eyes are sharp. You sit here on the Big Rock until you see Farmer Brown's boy coming. Then go hide in the bulrushes

[24]

where you can watch him, but where he cannot see you. Follow him everywhere he goes around the Smiling Pool or along the Laughing Brook. Without knowing it, he will show you where every trap is hidden.

"When all the traps have been found, drop a stick or a stone in each. That will spring them, and then they will be harmless. Then you can bury them deep in the mud. But don't eat any of the food until you have sprung all of the traps, for just as likely as not you will get caught. When all the traps have been sprung, why not bring all the good things to eat which you find around them to the Big

Billy Mink climbed up on the Big Rock to watch

Rock and have a grand feast?"

"Hurrah for Grandfather Frog! That's a great idea!" shouted Little Joe Otter, turning a somersault in the water.

Everyone agreed with Little Joe Otter, and immediately they began to plan a grand hunt for the traps of Farmer Brown's boy. The Muskrats and the Otters started to search the banks of the Smiling Pool, and the Coons and the Minks, all but Billy, started for the Laughing Brook. Billy climbed up on the Big Rock to watch, and Grandfather Frog slowly swam back to his big green lily pad to wait for some foolish green flies for his breakfast.

V

A Busy Day at the Smiling Pool

EVERYBODY was excited. Yes, Sir, everybody in the Smiling Pool and along the Laughing Brook was just bubbling over with excitement. Even Spotty the Turtle, who usually takes everything so calmly that some people think him stupid, climbed up on the highest point of an old log where he could see what was going on.

Only Grandfather Frog, sitting on his big green lily pad and watching for foolish green flies for his breakfast, appeared not to know that something unusual was going on. Really, he was just as much excited as the rest, but because he is very old and accounted very, very wise, it would not do for him to show it.

What was it all about? Why, all the Minks and the Coons and the Otters and the Muskrats, who live and play around the Smiling Pool and the Laughing Brook, were hunting for traps set by Farmer Brown's boy, just as Grandfather Frog had advised them to.

Jerry Muskrat and Little Joe Otter were hunting together. They were swimming along close to shore just where the Laughing Brook leaves the Smiling Pool, when Jerry wrinkled up his funny little nose and stopped swimming. Sniff, sniff, sniff, went Jerry Muskrat. Then little cold shivers ran down his backbone and way out to the tip of his tail.

"What is it?" asked Little Joe Otter.

"It's the man-smell," whispered Jerry. Just then Little Joe Otter gave a long sniff. "My, I smell fish!" he cried, his eyes sparkling, and started in the direction from which the smell came. He swam faster than Jerry, and in a minute he shouted in delight.

"Hi, Jerry! Someone's left a fish on the edge of the bank. What a feast!"

Jerry hurried as fast as he could swim, his eyes popping out with fright, for the nearer he got, the stronger grew that dreadful man-smell. "Don't touch it," he panted. "Don't touch it, Joe Otter!"

Little Joe laughed. "What's the matter, Jerry? 'Fraid I'll eat it all up before you get here?" he asked, as he reached out for the fish.

"Stop!" shrieked Jerry, and gave Little Joe a push, just as the latter touched the fish.

Snap! A pair of wicked steel

jaws flew together and caught Little Joe Otter by a claw of one toe. If it hadn't been for Jerry's push, he would have been caught by a foot.

"Oh! Oh! Oh!" cried Little Joe Otter.

"Next time I guess you'll remember what Grandfather Frog said about watching out when you find things to eat where they never were before," said Jerry, as he helped Little Joe pull himself free from the trap. But he left the claw behind and had a dreadfully sore toe as a result. Then they buried the trap deep down in the mud and started to look for another.

All around the Smiling Pool and

[*32*]

along the Laughing Brook their cousins and uncles and aunts and friends were just as busy, and every once in a while someone would have just as narrow an escape as Little Joe Otter. And all the time up at the farmhouse Farmer Brown's boy was planning what he would do with the skins of the little animals he was sure he would catch in his traps.

VI

Farmer Brown's Boy Is Puzzled

FARMER BROWN'S boy was whistling merrily as he tramped down across the Green Meadows. The Merry Little Breezes saw him coming, and they raced over to the Smiling Pool to tell Billy Mink. Farmer Brown's boy was coming to visit his traps. He was very sure that he would find Billy Mink or

Little Joe Otter, or Jerry Muskrat, or perhaps Bobby Coon.

Billy Mink was sitting on top of the Big Rock. He saw the Merry Little Breezes racing across the Green Meadows, and behind them he saw Farmer Brown's boy. Billy Mink dived headfirst into the Smiling Pool. Then he swam over to Jerry Muskrat's house and warned Jerry. Together they hunted up Little Joe Otter, and then the three little scamps in brown hid in the bulrushes, where they could watch Farmer Brown's boy.

The first place Farmer Brown's boy visited was Jerry Muskrat's old log. Very cautiously he peeped over the edge of the bank. The trap was gone!

"Hurrah!" shouted Farmer Brown's boy. He was very much excited, as he caught hold of the end of the chain, which fastened it to the old log. He was sure that at last he had caught Jerry Muskrat. When he pulled the trap up, it was empty. Between the jaws were a few hairs and little bit of skin, which Jerry Muskrat had left there when he sprung the trap with his tail.

Farmer Brown's boy was disappointed. "Well, I'll get him tomorrow, anyway," said he to himself. Then he went on to his next trap;

it was nowhere to be seen. When he pulled the chain he was so excited that he trembled. The trap did not come up at once. He pulled and pulled, and then suddenly up it came, all covered with mud. In it was one little claw from Little Joe Otter. Very carefully Farmer Brown's boy set the trap again. If he could have looked over in the bulrushes and have seen Little Joe Otter and Billy Mink and Jerry Muskrat watching him and tickling and laughing, he would not have been so sure that next time he would catch Little Joe Otter.

All around the Smiling Pool and then up and down the Laughing Brook Farmer Brown's boy tramped, and each trap he found sprung and buried in the mud. He had stopped whistling by this time, and there was a puzzled frown on his freckled face. What did it mean? Could some other boy have found all his traps and played a trick by springing all of them? The more he thought about it, the more puzzled he became. You see, he did not know anything about the busy day the Minks and the Otters and the Muskrats and the Coons had spent the day before.

Old Grandfather Frog, sitting on his big green lily pad, smoothed down his white and yellow waistcoat and winked up at jolly, round, red Mr. Sun as Farmer Brown's boy tramped off across the Green Meadows.

"Chugarum!" said Grandfather Frog, as he snapped up a foolish green fly. "Much good it will do you to set those traps again!"

Then Grandfather Frog called to Billy Mink and sent him to tell all the other little people of the Smiling Pool and the Laughing Brook that they must hurry and spring all the traps again as they had before.

This time it was easy, because they knew just where the traps were, so all day long they dropped sticks and stones into the traps and once more sprung them. Then they prepared for a grand feast of the good things to eat which Farmer Brown's boy had left scattered around the traps.

VII

Jerry Muskrat Makes a Discovery

THE beautiful springtime had brought a great deal of happiness to the Smiling Pool, as it had to the Green Meadows and to the Green Forest. Great-Grandfather Frog, who had slept the long winter away in his own special bed way down in the mud, had waked up with an appetite so great that for a while it seemed as if he could think of nothing but his stomach. Jerry Muskrat had felt the spring fever in his bones and had gone up and down the Laughing Brook, poking into all kinds of places just for the fun of seeing new things. Little Joe Otter had been more full of fun than ever, if that were possible. Mr. and Mrs. Redwing had come back to the bulrushes from their winter home way down in the warm Southland. Everybody was happy, just as happy as could be.

One sunny morning Jerry Muskrat sat on the Big Rock in the middle of the Smiling Pool, just thinking of how happy everybody was and laughing at Little Joe Otter, who was cutting up all sorts of capers in the water. Suddenly Jerry's sharp eyes saw something that made him wrinkle his forehead in a puzzled frown and look and look at the opposite bank. Finally he called to Little Joe Otter.

"Hi, Little Joe! Come over here!" shouted Jerry.

"What for?" asked Little Joe, turning a somersault in the water.

"I want you to see if there is anything wrong with my eyes," replied Jerry.

Little Joe Otter stopped swimming and stared up at Jerry Musk-rat. "They look all right to me,"

"Hi, Little Joe! Come over here!" shouted Jerry

said he, as he started to climb up on the Big Rock.

"Of course they look all right," replied Jerry, "but what I want to know is if they see all right. Look over at that bank."

Little Joe Otter looked over at the bank. He stared and stared, but he didn't see anything unusual. It looked just as it always did. He told Jerry Muskrat so.

"Then it must be my eyes," sighed Jerry. "It certainly must be my eyes. It looks to me as if the water does not come as high up on the bank as it did yesterday."

Little Joe Otter looked again and his eyes opened wide. "You are right, Jerry Muskrat!" he cried. "There's nothing the matter with your eyes. The water is as low as it ever gets, even in the very middle of summer. What can it mean?"

"I don't know," replied Jerry Muskrat. "It is queer! It certainly is very queer! Let's go ask Grandfather Frog. You know he is very old and very wise, so perhaps he can tell us what it means."

Splash! Jerry Muskrat and Little Joe Otter dived into the Smiling Pool and started a race to see who could reach Grandfather Frog first. He was sitting among the bulrushes on the edge of the Smiling Pool, for the lily pads were not yet big

enough for him to sit on comfortably.

"Oh, Grandfather Frog, what's
the matter with the Smiling Pool?"
they shouted, as they came up quite
out of breath.

"Chugarum! There's nothing
the matter with the Smiling Pool;
it's the best place in all the
world," replied Grandfather Frog
gruffly.

"But there is something the
matter," insisted Jerry Muskrat,
and then he told what he had
discovered.

"I don't believe it," said
Grandfather Frog. "I never heard
of such a thing in springtime."

[47]

VIII

Grandfather Frog Watches His Toes

GRANDFATHER FROG sat among the bulrushes on the edge of the Smiling Pool. Over his head Mr. Redwing was singing as if his heart would burst with the very joy of springtime:

> "Tra-la-la-lee, see me! See me!
> Happy am I as I can be!
> Happy am I the whole day long
> And so I sing my gladsome song."

Of course Mr. Redwing was happy. Why shouldn't he be? Here it was the beautiful springtime, the gladdest time of all the year, the time when happiness creeps into everybody's heart. Grandfather Frog listened. He nodded his head. "Chugarum! I'm happy, too," said Grandfather Frog. But even as he said it, a little worried look crept into his big goggly eyes and then down to the corners of his big mouth, which had been stretched in a smile. Little by little the smile grew smaller and smaller, until there wasn't any smile. No, Sir, there wasn't any smile. Instead of looking happy, as he said he felt,

Grandfather Frog actually looked unhappy.

The fact is, he couldn't forget what Jerry Muskrat and Little Joe Otter had told him—that there was something the matter with the Smiling Pool. He didn't believe it, not a word of it. At least he tried to make himself think that he didn't believe it. They had said that the water in the Smiling Pool was growing lower and lower, just as it did in the middle of summer, in the very hottest weather. Now Grandfather Frog is very old and very wise, and he had never heard of such a thing happening in the

[50]

springtime. So he wouldn't believe it now. And yet—and yet Grandfather Frog had an uncomfortable feeling that something was wrong. Ha! he knew now what it was! He had been sitting up to his middle in water, and now he was sitting with only his toes in the water, and he couldn't remember having changed his position!

"Of course, I moved without thinking what I was doing," muttered Grandfather Frog, but still the worried look didn't leave his face. You see, he just couldn't make himself believe what he wanted to believe, try as he would.

[51]

"Chugarum! I know what I'll do; I'll watch my toes!" exclaimed Grandfather Frog.

So Grandfather Frog waded out into the water until it covered his feet, and then he sat down and began to watch his toes. Mr. Redwing looked down and saw him, and Grandfather Frog looked so funny gazing at his own toes that Mr. Redwing stopped singing long enough to ask:

"What are you doing, Grandfather Frog?"

"Watching my toes," replied Grandfather Frog gruffly.

"Watching your toes! Ho, ho, ho! Watching your toes! Whoever heard of such a thing? Are you afraid that they will run away, Grandfather Frog?" shouted Mr. Redwing.

Grandfather Frog didn't answer. He kept right on watching his toes. Mr. Redwing flew away to tell everybody he met how Grandfather Frog had become foolish and was watching his toes. The sun shone down warm and bright, and pretty soon Grandfather Frog's big goggly eyes began to blink. Then his head began to nod, and then—why, then Grandfather Frog fell fast asleep.

By and by Grandfather Frog awoke with a start. He looked down at his toes. They were not in the water at all! Indeed, the water was a good long jump away.

"Chugarum! There is something wrong with the Smiling Pool!" cried Grandfather Frog, as he made a long jump into the water and started to swim out to the Big Rock.

IX

The Laughing Brook Stops Laughing

THERE was something wrong. Grandfather Frog knew it the very minute he got up that morning. At first he couldn't think what it was. He sat with just his head out of water and blinked his great goggly eyes, as he tried to think what it was that was wrong. Suddenly Grandfather Frog realized how still it was. It was a different kind of stillness from anything he could remember. He missed something, and he couldn't think what it was. It wasn't the song of Mr. Redwing. There were many times when he didn't hear that. It was—Grandfather Frog gave a startled jump out on to the shore. "Chugarum! It's the Laughing Brook! The Laughing Brook has stopped laughing!" cried Grandfather Frog.

Could it be? Whoever heard of such a thing, excepting when Jack Frost bound the Laughing Brook with hard black ice? Why, in the spring and in the summer and in the fall the Laughing Brook had

"The Laughing Brook has stopped laughing!"
Grandfather Frog cried

laughed—such a merry, happy laugh—ever since Grandfather Frog could remember, and you know he can remember way back in the long ago, for he is very old and very wise. Never once in all that time had the Laughing Brook failed to laugh. It couldn't be true now! Grandfather Frog put a hand behind one ear and listened and listened, but not a sound could he hear.

"Chugarum! It must be me," said Grandfather Frog. "It must be that I am growing old and deaf. I'll go over and ask Jerry Muskrat."

So Grandfather Frog dived into the water and swam out to the middle of the Smiling Pool, on his way to Jerry Muskrat's house. It was then that he first fully realized the truth of what Jerry Muskrat and Little Joe Otter had told him the day before—that there was something very, very wrong with the Smiling Pool. He stopped swimming to look around, and it seemed as if his great goggly eyes would pop right out of his head. Yes, Sir, it seemed as if those great goggly eyes certainly would pop right out of Grandfather Frog's head. The Smiling Pool had grown so small that there wasn't enough of it left to smile!

"Where are you going, Grandfather Frog?" asked a voice over his head.

Grandfather Frog looked up.

Looking down on him from over the edge of the Big Rock was Jerry Muskrat. The edge of the Big Rock was twice as high above the water as Grandfather Frog had ever seen it before.

"I—I—was going to swim over to your house to see you," replied Grandfather Frog.

"It's of no use," replied Jerry, "because I'm not there. Besides, you couldn't swim there, anyway."

"Why not?" demanded Grandfather Frog in great surprise.

"Because it isn't in the water any longer; it's way up on dry land," said Jerry Muskrat in the most mournful voice.

"What's that you say?" cried Grandfather Frog, as if he couldn't believe his own ears.

"It's just as true as that I'm sitting here," replied Jerry sadly.

"Listen, Jerry Muskrat, and tell me truly; is the Laughing Brook laughing?" cried Grandfather Frog sharply.

"No," replied Jerry, "the Laughing Brook has stopped laughing, and the Smiling Pool has stopped smiling, and I think the world is upside down."

X

Why the World Seemed Upside Down to Jerry Muskrat

JERRY MUSKRAT sat on the Big Rock in the Smiling Pool, which smiled no longer, and held his head in both hands, for his head ached. He had thought and thought, until it seemed to him that his head would split; and with all his thinking, he didn't understand things any more now than he had in the beginning. You see, Jerry Muskrat's little world was topsy-turvy. Yes, Sir, Jerry's world was upside down! Anyway, it seemed so to him, and he couldn't understand it at all.

The Smiling Pool, the Laughing Brook, and the Green Meadows are Jerry Muskrat's little world. Now, as he sat on the Big Rock and looked about him, the Green Meadows were as lovely as ever. He could see no change in them. But the Laughing Brook had stopped laughing, and the Smiling Pool had stopped smiling. The truth is, there wasn't enough of the Laughing Brook left to laugh, and there wasn't enough of the Smiling Pool left to smile.

It was dreadful! Jerry looked over to his house, of which he had once been so proud. He had built it with the doorway under water. He had felt perfectly safe there, because no one excepting Billy Mink or Little Joe Otter, who can swim under water, could reach him. Now the Smiling Pool had grown so small that Jerry's house wasn't in the water at all. Anybody who wanted to could get into it. There was the doorway plainly to be seen. Worse

[*64*]

still, there was the secret entrance
to the long tunnel leading to his
castle under the roots of the Big
Hickory Tree. That had been
Jerry's most secret secret, and now
there it was for all the world to see.
And there were all the wonderful
caves and holes and hiding places
under the bank which had been
known only to Jerry Muskrat and
Billy Mink and Little Joe Otter, because the openings had always been
under water. Now, anybody could
find them, for they were plainly to
be seen. And where had always
been smiling, dimpling water, Jerry
saw only mud. It was mud, mud,
mud everywhere! The bulrushes,

It was mud, mud, mud everywhere!

which had always grown with their feet in the water, now had them only in mud, and that was fast drying up. The lily pads lay half curled up at the ends of their long stems, stretched out on the mud, and looked very, very sick. Jerry turned toward the Laughing Brook. There was just a little teeny, weeny stream of water trickling down the middle of it, with here and there a tiny pool in which frightened trout and minnows were crowded. All the secrets of the Laughing Brook were exposed, just as were the secrets of the Smiling Pool. Jerry knew that if he wanted to find Billy Mink's hiding places,

[67]

all he need do would be to walk up the Laughing Brook and look.

"Yes, Sir, the world has turned upside down," said Jerry in a mournful voice.

"I believe it has," replied Grandfather Frog, looking up from the little pool of water left at the foot of the Big Rock.

"I know it has!" cried Jerry. "I wonder if it will ever turn upside up again."

"If it doesn't, what are you going to do?" asked Grandfather Frog.

"I don't know," replied Jerry Muskrat. "Here come Little Joe Otter and Billy Mink; let's find out what they are going to do."

XI

Five Heads Together

SOMETHING had to be done. Jerry Muskrat said so. Grandfather Frog said so. Billy Mink said so. Little Joe Otter said so. Even Spotty the Turtle said so. The Laughing Brook couldn't laugh, and the Smiling Pool couldn't smile. You see, there wasn't water enough in either of them to laugh or smile, and nobody knew if there ever would be again. Nobody had ever known anything like it before, and so nobody knew what to think or do. And yet they all felt that something must be done.

"What do you think, Billy Mink?" asked Grandfather Frog.

Billy Mink looked down from the top of the Big Rock into the little pool of water that was all there was left of the Smiling Pool. He could see a dozen fat trout in it, and he knew that he could catch them just as easily as not, because there was no place for them to swim away from him. But somehow he didn't want to catch them. He knew that they were frightened almost to death already by the running away of nearly all the water from the Laughing Brook and the Smiling Pool, and somehow he felt sorry for them.

"I think that the best thing we can do is to move down to the Big River. I've been down there, and that's all right," said Billy Mink.

"That's what I think," said Little Joe Otter. "There's no danger that the Big River will go dry."

"How do you know?" asked Jerry Muskrat. "The Laughing Brook and the Smiling Pool never went dry before."

"It's a long, long way down to the Big River," broke in Spotty the Turtle, who travels very, very slowly and carries his house with him.

"Chugarum! I, for one, don't want to leave the Smiling Pool without finding out what the trouble is.

"There's nothing happens, as you know,
But has a cause to make it so.

"Now there must be some cause, some reason, for this terrible trouble with the Smiling Pool, and if we can find that out, perhaps we shall know better what to do," said Grandfather Frog.

Jerry Muskrat nodded his head. "Grandfather Frog is right," said he. "Of course there must be a cause, but where are we to look for it? I've been all over the Smiling

[72]

Pool, and I'm sure it isn't there."

Grandfather Frog actually smiled. "Chugarum!" said he. "Of course the cause of all the trouble isn't in the Smiling Pool. Anyone would know that!"

"Well, if you know so much, tell us where it is then!" snapped Jerry Muskrat.

"In the Laughing Brook, of course," replied Grandfather Frog.

"No such thing!" said Billy Mink. "I've been all the way down the Laughing Brook to the Big River, and I didn't find a thing."

"Have you been all the way up the Laughing Brook to the place it

[73]

starts from?" asked Grandfather Frog.

"No-o," replied Billy Mink.

"Well, that's where the cause of all the trouble is," said Grandfather Frog, just as if he knew all about it. "It's the water that comes down the Laughing Brook that makes the Smiling Pool, and the Smiling Pool never could dry up if the Laughing Brook didn't first stop running."

"That's so! I never had thought of that," cried Little Joe Otter. "I tell you what, Billy Mink and I will go way up the Laughing Brook and see what we can find."

"Chugarum! Let us all go," said Grandfather Frog.

[74]

FIVE HEADS TOGETHER

Then the five put their heads together and decided that they would
go up the Laughing Brook to hunt
for the trouble.

XII

A Hunt for Trouble

O L' MISTAH BUZZARD, sailing high in the blue, blue sky, looked down on a funny sight. Yes, Sir, it certainly was a funny sight. It was a little procession of five of his friends of the Smiling Pool. First was Billy Mink, who, because he is slim and nimble, moves so quickly it sometimes is hard to follow him. Behind him was Little Joe Otter, whose legs are so short that he almost looks as if he hadn't any. Behind Little Joe was Jerry Muskrat, who is a better traveler in the water than on land. Behind Jerry was Grandfather Frog, who neither walks nor runs but travels with great jumps. Last of all was Spotty the Turtle, who travels very, very slowly because, you know, he carries his house with him. And all five were headed up the Laughing Brook, which laughed no more, because there was not water enough in it.

Now Ol' Mistah Buzzard hadn't been over near the Smiling Pool for some time, and he hadn't heard how the Smiling Pool had stopped smiling, and the Laughing Brook had stopped laughing. When he looked down and saw how the water was so nearly gone from them that the trout and the minnows had hardly enough in which to live, he was so surprised that he kept saying over and over to himself:

"Fo' the lan's sake! Fo' the lan's sake!"

Then, when he saw his five little friends marching up the Laughing Brook, he guessed right away that it must be something to do with the trouble in the Smiling Pool. Ol' Mistah Buzzard just turned his broad wings and slid down, down out of the blue, blue sky until he was right over Grandfather Frog.

Ol' Mistah Buzzard slid down out of the blue,
blue sky

"Where are yo'alls going?" asked Ol' Mistah Buzzard.

"Chugarum! To find out what is the trouble with the Laughing Brook," replied Grandfather Frog.

"I'll help you," said Ol' Mistah Buzzard, once more sailing up in the blue, blue sky.

Grandfather Frog watched him until he was nothing but a speck. "I wish I had wings," sighed Grandfather Frog, and once more began to hop along up the bed of the Laughing Brook.

The Laughing Brook came down from the Green Forest and wound through the Green Meadows for a little way before it reached the Smiling Pool. There the sun shone down into it, and Grandfather Frog didn't mind, although his legs were getting tired. But when they got into the Green Forest it was dark and gloomy. At least Grandfather Frog thought so, and so did Spotty the Turtle, for both dearly love the sunshine. But still they kept on, for they felt that they must find the trouble with the Laughing Brook. If they found this, they would also find the trouble with the Smiling Pool.

So Billy Mink jumped and skipped far ahead; Little Joe Otter ran; Jerry Muskrat walked, for he soon gets tired on land; Grandfather Frog hopped; Spotty the Turtle crawled, and way, way up in the blue, blue sky, Ol' Mistah Buzzard flew, all looking for the trouble which had stopped the laughing of the Laughing Brook and the smiling of the Smiling Pool.

XIII

Ol' Mistah Buzzard
Sees Something

WAIT for me!" cried Little Joe Otter to Billy Mink, but Billy Mink was in too much of a hurry and just ran faster.

"Wait for me!" cried Jerry Muskrat to Little Joe Otter, but Little Joe was in too much of a hurry and just ran faster.

"Wait for me!" cried Grandfather

Frog to Jerry Muskrat, but Jerry was in too much of a hurry and just walked faster.

"Wait for me!" cried Spotty the Turtle to Grandfather Frog, but Grandfather Frog was in too much of a hurry and just jumped faster.

So running and walking and jumping and crawling, Billy Mink, Little Joe Otter, Jerry Muskrat, Grandfather Frog, and Spotty the Turtle hurried up the Laughing Brook to try to find out why it laughed no more. And high overhead in the blue, blue sky sailed Ol' Mistah Buzzard, and he also was looking for the trouble that had taken away the laugh from the

[84]

Laughing Brook and the smile from the Smiling Pool.

Now Ol' Mistah Buzzard's eyes are very sharp, and looking down from way up in the blue, blue sky he can see a great deal. Indeed, Ol' Mistah Buzzard can see all that is going on below on the Green Meadows and in the Green Forest. His wings are very broad, and he can sail through the air very swiftly when he makes up his mind to. Now, as he looked down, he saw that Billy Mink was selfish and wouldn't wait for Little Joe Otter, and Little Joe Otter was selfish and wouldn't wait for Jerry Muskrat, and Jerry Muskrat was selfish and wouldn't wait for Grandfather Frog, and Grandfather Frog was selfish and wouldn't wait for Spotty the Turtle.

"Ah reckon Ah will hurry up right smart and find out what the trouble is mahself, and then go back and tell Brer Turtle; it will save him a powerful lot of work, and it will serve Brer Mink right if Brer Turtle finds out first what is the trouble with the Laughing Brook," said Ol' Mistah Buzzard and shot far ahead over the Green Forest toward that part of it from which the Laughing Brook comes. In a few minutes he was as far ahead of

Billy Mink as Billy was ahead of
Spotty the Turtle.

For wings are swifter far than legs,
On whatsoever purpose bent,
But doubly swift and tireless
Those wings on kindly deed intent.

And this is how it happened that
Ol' Mistah Buzzard was the first to
find out what it was that had
stopped the laughing of the Laughing Brook and the smiling of the
Smiling Pool, but he was so surprised when he did find out that he
forgot all about going back to tell
Spotty the Turtle. He forgot everything but his own great surprise,
and he blinked his eyes a great

[87]

Then he sailed around and around in circles

many times to make sure that he wasn't dreaming. Then he sailed around and around in circles, looking down among the trees of the Green Forest and saying over and over to himself:

"Did yo' ever? No, Ah never! Did yo' ever? No, Ah never!"

XIV

Spotty the Turtle Keeps Right On Going

"One step, two steps, three steps, so!
Four steps, five steps, six steps go!
Keep right on and do your best;
Mayhap you'll win while others rest."

SPOTTY THE TURTLE said this over to himself every time he felt a little downhearted, as he plodded along the bed of the

Laughing Brook. And every time he said it, he felt better. "One step, two steps," he kept saying over and over, and each time he said it, he took a step and then another. They were very short steps, very short steps indeed, for Spotty's legs are very short. But each one carried him forward just so much, and he knew that he was just so much nearer the thing he was seeking. Anyway, he hoped he was.

You see, if the Laughing Brook would never laugh any more, and the Smiling Pool would never smile any more, there was nothing to do but to go down to the Big River to live, and no one wanted to do that, especially Grandfather Frog and Spotty the Turtle.

Now, because Billy Mink could go faster than Little Joe Otter, and Little Joe Otter could go faster than Jerry Muskrat, and Jerry could go faster than Grandfather Frog, and Grandfather Frog could go faster than Spotty the Turtle, and because each one wanted to be the first to find the trouble, no one would wait for the one behind him. So Spotty the Turtle, who has to carry his house with him, was a long, long way behind the others. But he kept right on going.

"One step, two steps, three steps, so!"

and he didn't stop for anything. He crawled over sticks and around big stones and sometimes, when he found a little pool of water, he swam. He always felt better then, because he can swim faster than he can walk.

After a long, long time, Spotty the Turtle came to a little pool where the sunshine lay warm and inviting. There, in the middle of it, on a mossy stone, sat Grandfather Frog fast asleep. He had thought that he was so far ahead of Spotty that he could safely rest his tired legs. Spotty wanted to climb right up beside him and take a nap

[93]

*There, on a mossy stone, sat Grandfather Frog
fast asleep*

too, but he didn't. He just grinned to himself and kept right on going.

"One step, two steps, three steps, so!"

while Grandfather Frog slept on.

By and by, after a long, long time, Spotty came to another little pool, and who should he see but Jerry Muskrat busily opening and eating some fresh-water clams which he had found there. He was so busy enjoying himself that he didn't see Spotty, and Spotty didn't say a word, but kept right on going, although the sight of Jerry's feast had made him dreadfully hungry.

By and by, after a long, long time, he came to a third little pool with a high, smooth bank, and who should he see there but Little Joe Otter, who had made a slippery slide down the smooth bank and was having a glorious time sliding down into the little pool. Spotty would have liked to take just one slide, but he didn't. He didn't even let Little Joe Otter see him, but kept right on going.

"One step, two steps, three steps, so!"

By and by, after a long, long time, he came to a hollow log, and just happening to peep in, he saw someone curled up fast asleep. Who was it? Why, Billy Mink, to be sure! You see, Billy thought that he was

[*96*]

so far ahead that he might just as well take it easy, and that was what he was doing. Spotty the Turtle didn't waken him. He just kept right on going the same slow way he had come all day, and so, just as jolly, round, red Mr. Sun was going to bed behind the Purple Hills, Spotty the Turtle found the cause of the trouble in the Laughing Brook and the Smiling Pool.

XV

What Spotty the Turtle Found

SPOTTY THE TURTLE stared and stared and stared, until it seemed as if his eyes surely would pop out of his funny little head. Of course he could believe his own eyes, and yet—and yet—well, if anybody else had seen what he was looking at and had told him about it, he wouldn't have believed it.

[98]

No, Sir, he wouldn't have believed it. You see, he couldn't have believed it because—why, because it didn't seem as if it could be really and truly so.

He wondered if the sun shining in his eyes made him think he saw more than he really did see, so he carefully changed his position. It made no difference. Then Spotty was sure that what he saw was real, and that he had found the cause of the trouble in the Laughing Brook, which had made it stop laughing and the Smiling Pool stop smiling.

Spotty the Turtle was feeling pretty good. In fact, Spotty was feeling very good indeed, because he had been the first to find out what was the matter with the Laughing Brook. At least, he thought that he was the first, and he was—of all the little people who lived in the Smiling Pool. Only Ol' Mistah Buzzard had been before him, and he didn't count because his wings are broad, and all he had to do was to sail over the Green Forest and look down. The ones who really counted were Billy Mink and Little Joe Otter and Jerry Muskrat and Grandfather Frog. Billy Mink had stopped for a nap. Little Joe Otter had stopped to play. Jerry Muskrat had stopped to eat. Grandfather Frog had stopped for a sun nap. But Spotty the Turtle had kept right on going, and now here he was, the first one to find the cause of the trouble in the Laughing Brook. Do you wonder that he felt proud and very happy?

Keeping at it, that's the way
Spotty won the race that day.

But now Spotty was beginning to wish that some of the others would hurry up. He wanted to know what they thought. He wanted to talk it all over. It was such a surprising thing that he could make neither head nor tail of it himself, and he wondered what the others would say. And now the long black shadows were creeping through the

Green Forest, and if they didn't get there pretty soon, they would have to wait until the next day.

So Spotty the Turtle found a good place to spend the night, and then he sat down to watch and wait. Right before him was the thing which he had found and which puzzled him so. What was it? Why, it was a wall. Yes, Sir, that is just what it was—a wall of logs and sticks and mud, and it was right across the Laughing Brook, where the banks were steep and narrow. Of course the Laughing Brook could laugh no longer; there couldn't enough water get through that wall of logs and sticks and mud to make even the beginning of a laugh. Spotty wondered what lay behind that wall, and who had built it, and what for, and a lot of other things. And he was still wondering when he fell asleep.

XVI

The Pond in the Green Forest

SPOTTY THE TURTLE was awake by the time the first rays of the rising sun began to creep through the Green Forest. He was far, far up the Laughing Brook, very much farther than he had ever been before, and as he yawned and stretched, he wondered if after all he hadn't dreamed about the wall of logs and sticks and mud across

He was far, far up the Laughing Brook

the Laughing Brook. When he had rubbed the last sleepy-wink out of his eyes, he looked again. There it was, just as he had seen it the night before! Then Spotty knew that it was real, and he began to wonder what was on the other side of it.

"I cannot climb it, for my legs were never made for climbing," said Spotty mournfully as he looked at his funny little black feet. "Oh dear, I wish that I could climb like Happy Jack Squirrel!" Just then a thought popped into his head and chased away the little frown that had crept into Spotty's face. "Perhaps

Happy Jack sometimes wishes that he could swim as I can, so I guess we are even. I can't climb, but he can't swim. How foolish it is to wish for things never meant for you!"

And with that, all the discontent left Spotty the Turtle, and he began to study how he could make the most of his short legs and his perseverance, of which, as you already know, he had a great deal. He looked this way and he looked that way, and he saw that if he could climb to the top of the bank on one side of the Laughing Brook, he would be able to walk right out on the strange wall of logs and sticks and mud, and then, of course, he could see just what was on the other side.

So Spotty the Turtle wasted no more time wishing that he could do something it was never meant that he should do. Instead, he picked out what looked like the easiest place to climb the bank and started up. My, my, my, it was hard work! You see, he had to carry his house along with him, for he has to carry that wherever he goes, and it would have been hard enough to have climbed that bank without carrying anything. Every time he had climbed up three steps he slipped back two steps, but he kept at it, puffing and blowing, saying over and over to himself:

"I can if I will, and will if I can!
I'm sure to get there if I follow this plan."

Halfway up the bank Spotty lost his balance, and the house he was carrying just tipped him right over backward, and down he rolled to the place he had started from.

"I needed to cool off," said Spotty to himself and slid into a little pool of water. Then he tried the bank again, and just as before he slipped back two steps for every three he went up. But he shut his mouth tight and kept at it, and by and by he was up to the place from which he had tumbled. There he stopped to get his breath.

"I can if I will, and will if I can!
I'm sure to get there if I follow this plan,"

said he and started on again. Twice more he tumbled clear down to the place he had started from, but each time he laughed at himself and tried again. And at last he reached the top of the bank.

"I said I could if I would, and I would if I could, and I have!" he cried.

Then he hurried to see what was

behind the strange wall. What do you think it was? Why, a pond! Yes, Sir, there was a pond right in the middle of the Green Forest! Trees were coming up right out of the middle of it, but it was a sure-enough pond. Spotty found it harder work to believe his own eyes now than when he had first seen the strange wall across the Laughing Brook.

"Why, why, why, what does it mean?" exclaimed Spotty the Turtle.

"That's what I want to know!" cried Billy Mink, who came hurrying up just then.

XVII

Who Had Made the Strange Pond?

WHO had made the strange pond? That is what Spotty the Turtle wanted to know. That is what Billy Mink wanted to know. So did Little Joe Otter and Jerry Muskrat and Grandfather Frog, when they arrived. So did Ol' Mistah Buzzard, looking down from the blue, blue sky. It was very strange, very strange indeed! Never had there been a pond in that part of the Green Forest before, not even in the days when Sister South Wind melted the snow so fast that the Laughing Brook ran over its banks and the Smiling Pool grew twice as large as it ought to be.

Of course someone had made it. Spotty the Turtle had known that as soon as he had seen the strange pond. All in a flash he had understood what that wall of logs and brush and mud across the Laughing Brook was for. It was to stop the water from running down the Laughing Brook. And of course, if the water couldn't keep on running and laughing on its way to the Smiling Pool, it would just stand still and grow and grow into a pond. Of course! There was nothing else for it to do. Spotty felt very proud when he had thought that out all by himself.

"This wall we are sitting on has made the pond," said Spotty the Turtle, after a long time in which no one had spoken.

"You don't say so!" said Billy Mink. "How ever, ever did you guess it? Are you sure, quite sure, that the pond didn't make the wall?"

Spotty knew that Billy Mink was making fun of him, but he is too good-natured to lose his temper over a little thing like that. He tried to think of something smart to say in reply, but Spotty is a slow thinker as well as a slow walker, and before he could think of anything, Billy was talking once more.

"This wall is what Farmer Brown's boy calls a dam," said Billy Mink, who is a great traveler. "Dams are usually built to keep water from running where it isn't wanted or to make it go where it is wanted, Now, what I want to know is, who under the sun wants a pond way back here in the Green

*"Of course," said Little Joe Otter, as if he knew
all about it*

Forest, and what is it for? Who do you think built this dam, Grandfather Frog?"

Grandfather Frog shook his head. His big goggly eyes seemed more goggly than ever, as he stared at the new pond in the Green Forest.

"I don't know," said Grandfather Frog. "I don't know what to think."

"Why, it must be Farmer Brown's boy or Farmer Brown himself," said Jerry Muskrat.

"Of course," said Little Joe Otter, just as if he knew all about it.

Still Grandfather Frog shook his head, as if he didn't agree. "I

[117]

don't know," said Grandfather Frog, "I don't know. It doesn't look so to me."

Billy Mink ran along the top of the dam and down the back side. He looked it all over with those sharp little eyes of his.

"Grandfather Frog is right," said he, when he came back. "It doesn't look like the work of Farmer Brown or Farmer Brown's boy. But if they didn't do it, who did? Who could have done it?"

"I don't know," said Grandfather Frog again, in a dreamy sort of voice.

Spotty the Turtle looked at him, and saw that Grandfather Frog's face wore the faraway look that it always does when he tells a story of the days when the world was young. "I don't know," he repeated, "but it looks to me very much like the work of—" Grandfather Frog stopped short off and turned to Jerry Muskrat. "Jerry Muskrat," said he, so sharply that Jerry nearly lost his balance in his surprise, "has your big cousin come down from the North?"

XVIII

Jerry Muskrat's Big Cousin

Fiddle, faddle, feedle, fuddle!
Was there ever such a muddle?
Fuddle, feedle, faddle, fiddle!
Who is there will solve the riddle?

HERE was the Laughing Brook laughing no longer. Here was the Smiling Pool smiling no longer. Here was a brand-new pond deep in the Green Forest. Here was a wall of logs and bushes and mud called a dam, built by someone whom nobody had seen. And here was Grandfather Frog asking Jerry Muskrat if his big cousin had come down from the North, when Jerry didn't even know that he had a big cousin.

"I—I haven't any big cousin," said Jerry, when he had quite recovered from his surprise at Grandfather Frog's question.

"Chugarum!" exclaimed Grandfather Frog, and the scornful way in which he said it made Jerry feel very small. "Chugarum! Of course you've got a big cousin in the North. Do you mean to tell me that you don't know that, Jerry Muskrat?"

Jerry had to admit that it was true that he didn't know anything about that big cousin. If Grandfather Frog said that he had one, it must be so, for Grandfather Frog is very old and very wise, and he knows a great deal. Still, it was very hard for Jerry to believe that he had a big cousin of whom he had never heard.

"Did—did you ever see him, Grandfather Frog?" Jerry asked.

"No!" snapped Grandfather Frog. "I never did, but I know all about him. He is a great worker, is this big cousin of yours, and he builds dams like this one we are sitting on."

"I don't believe it!" cried Billy

Mink. "I don't believe any cousin of Jerry Muskrat's ever built such a dam as this. Why, just look at that great tree trunk at the bottom! No one but Farmer Brown or Farmer Brown's boy could ever have dragged that there. You're crazy, Grandfather Frog, just plain crazy." Billy Mink sometimes is very disrespectful to Grandfather Frog.

"Chugarum!" replied Grandfather Frog. "I'm pretty old, but I'm not too old to learn, as some folks seem to be," and he looked very hard at Billy Mink. "Did I say that that tree trunk was dragged here?"

"No," replied Billy Mink, "but

if it wasn't dragged here, how did it get here? You are so smart, Grandfather Frog, tell me that!"

Grandfather Frog blinked his great goggly eyes at Billy Mink as he said, just as if he was very, very sorry for Billy, "Your eyes are very bright and very sharp, Billy Mink, and it is a great pity that you have never learned how to use them. That tree wasn't dragged here; it was cut so that it fell right where it lies." As he spoke, Grandfather Frog pointed to the stump of the tree, and Billy Mink saw that he was right.

But Billy Mink is like a great many other people; he dearly

[*124*]

loves to have the last word. Now he suddenly began to laugh.

"Ha, ha, ha! Ho, ho, ho!" laughed Billy Mink. "Ho, ho, ho! Ha, ha, ha!"

"What is it that is so funny?" snapped Grandfather Frog, for nothing makes him so angry as to be laughed at.

"Do you mean to say that any-body but Farmer Brown or Farmer Brown's boy could have cut down such a big tree as that?" asked Billy. "Why, that would be as hard as to drag the tree here."

"Jerry Muskrat's big cousin from the North could do it, and I be-lieve he did," replied Grandfather

Frog. "Now that we have found the cause of the trouble in the Laughing Brook and the Smiling Pool, what are we going to do about it?"

XIX

Jerry Muskrat Has a Busy Day

THERE was the strange pond in the Green Forest, and there was the dam of logs and sticks and mud which had made the strange pond, but look as they would, Billy Mink and Little Joe Otter and Jerry Muskrat and Grandfather Frog and Spotty the Turtle could see nothing of the one who had built the dam. It was very queer. The more they thought about it, the queerer it seemed. They looked this way, and they looked that way.

"There is one thing very sure, and that is that whoever built this dam had no thought for those who live in the Laughing Brook and the Smiling Pool," said Grandfather Frog. "They are selfish, just plain, every-day selfish; that's what they are! Now the Laughing Brook cannot laugh, and the Smiling Pool cannot smile, while this dam stops the water from running, and so—" Grandfather Frog stopped and looked around at his four friends.

"And so what?" cried Billy Mink impatiently.

"And so we must spoil this dam. We must make a place for the water to run through," said Grandfather Frog very gravely.

"Of course! That's the very thing!" cried Little Joe Otter and Billy Mink and Jerry Muskrat and Spotty the Turtle. Then Little Joe Otter looked at Billy Mink, and Billy Mink looked at Jerry Muskrat, and Jerry Muskrat looked at Spotty the Turtle, and after that they all looked very hard at Grandfather Frog, and all together they asked:

"How are we going to do it?"

[129]

Grandfather Frog scratched his head thoughtfully and looked a long time at the dam of logs and sticks and mud. Then his big mouth widened in a big smile.

"Why, that is very simple," said he. "Jerry Muskrat will make a big hole through the dam near the bottom, because he knows how, and the rest of us will keep watch to see that no harm comes near."

"The very thing!" cried Little Joe Otter and Billy Mink and Spotty the Turtle, but Jerry Muskrat thought it wasn't fair. You see, it gave him all of the real work to do. However, Jerry thought of his dear Smiling Pool, and how terrible it would be if it should smile no more, and so without another word he set to work.

Now Jerry Muskrat is a great worker, and he had made many long tunnels into the bank around the Smiling Pool, so he had no doubt but that he could soon make a hole through this dam. But almost right away he found trouble. Yes, Sir, Jerry had hardly begun before he found real trouble. You see, that dam was made mostly of sticks instead of mud, and so, instead of digging his way in as he would have done into the bank of the Smiling Pool, he had to stop every few minutes to gnaw off any sticks that were in the way.

It was hard work, the hardest kind of hard work. But Jerry Muskrat is the kind that is the more determined to do the work, the harder the work is to be done. And so, while Grandfather Frog sat on one end of the dam and pretended to keep watch, but really took a nap in the warm sunshine, and while Spotty the Turtle sat on the other end of the dam doing the same thing, and while Billy Mink and Little Joe Otter swam around in the strange pond and enjoyed themselves, Jerry Muskrat worked and worked and worked. And just as jolly, round, red Mr. Sun started down behind the Purple Hills, Jerry broke through into the strange pond, and the water began to run in the Laughing Brook once more.

XX

Jerry Has a Dreadful Disappointment

There's nothing in this world that's sure,
No matter how we scheme and plan.
We simply have to be content
With doing just the best we can.

JERRY MUSKRAT had curled himself up for the night, so tired
that he could hardly keep his eyes
open long enough to find a comfortable place to sleep. But he was
happy. Yes, indeed, Jerry was

[*134*]

happy. He could hear the Laughing Brook beginning to laugh again. It was just a little low, gurgling laugh, but Jerry knew that in a little while it would grow into the full laugh that makes music through the Green Forest and puts happiness into the hearts of all who hear it.

So Jerry was happy, for was it not because of him that the Laughing Brook was beginning to laugh? He had worked all the long day to make a hole through the dam which someone had built across the Laughing Brook and so stopped its laughter. Now the water was running again, and soon the new, strange pond behind the dam there in the Green Forest would be gone, and the Laughing Brook and the Smiling Pool would be their own beautiful selves once more. It was because he had worked so hard all day that he was going to sleep now. Usually he would rather sleep a part of the day and be abroad at night.

Very pleasant dreams had Jerry Muskrat that night, dreams of the dear Smiling Pool, smiling just as it had as long as Jerry could remember, before this trouble had come. He was still dreaming when Spotty the Turtle found him and waked him, for it was broad daylight.

Jerry yawned and stretched, and then he lay still for a minute to listen to the pleasant murmur of the Laughing Brook. But there wasn't any pleasant murmur. There wasn't any sound at all. Jerry began to wonder if he really was awake after all. He looked at Spotty the Turtle, and he knew then that he was, for Spotty's face had such a worried look.

"Get up, Jerry Muskrat, and come look at the hole you made yesterday in the dam. You couldn't have done your work very well, for the hole has filled up so that the water does not run any more," said Spotty.

"I did do it well!" snapped Jerry crossly. "I did it just as well as I know how. You lazy folks who just sit and take sun naps while you pretend to keep watch had better get busy and do a little work yourselves, if you don't like the way I work."

"I—I beg your pardon, Jerry Muskrat. I didn't mean to say just that," replied Spotty. "You see, we are all worried. We thought last night that by this morning the Laughing Brook would be full of water again, and we could go back to the Smiling Pool as soon as we felt like it, and here it is as bad as ever."

"Perhaps the trouble is just that some sticks and grass drifted down in the water and filled up the hole I made; that must be the trouble," said Jerry hopefully, as he hurried toward the dam.

First he carefully examined it from the Laughing Brook side. Then he dived down under water on the other side. He was gone a long time, and Billy Mink was just getting ready to dive to see what had become of him when he came up again.

"What is the trouble?" cried Spotty the Turtle and Grandfather Frog and Billy Mink and Little Joe Otter together. "Is the hole filled up with stuff that has drifted in?"

Jerry shook his head, as he slowly climbed out of the water. "No," said he. "No, it isn't filled with drift stuff brought down by the water. It is filled with sticks and mud that somebody has put there. Somebody has filled up the hole that I worked so hard to make yesterday, and it will take me all day to open it up again."

Then Grandfather Frog and Spotty the Turtle and Billy Mink and Little Joe Otter and Jerry Muskrat stared at one another, and for a long time no one said a word.

XXI

Jerry Muskrat
Keeps Watch

"The way in which to find things out,
And what goes on all round about,
Is just to keep my two eyes peeled
And two ears all the time unsealed."

SO SAID Jerry Muskrat, as he
settled himself comfortably on
one end of the new dam across
the Laughing Brook deep in the
Green Forest, and watched the dark
shadows creep farther and farther

out into the strange pond made by the new dam.

"I'm going to find out who it is that built this dam, and who it is that filled the hole I made in it! I'm going to find out if I have to move up here and live all summer!" The way in which Jerry said this and snapped his teeth together showed that he meant just what he said.

You see, Jerry had spent another long, weary day opening the hole in the dam once more, only to have it closed again while he slept. That had been enough for Jerry. He hadn't tried again. Instead, he had made up his mind that he would find out who was playing such a trick on him. He would just watch until they came, and then if they were not bigger than he, or there were not too many of them, he would—well, the way Jerry gritted and clashed those sharp teeth of his sounded as if he meant to do something pretty bad.

Billy Mink and Little Joe Otter had given up in disgust and started for the Big River. They are great travelers, anyway, and so didn't mind so much because there was no longer water enough in the Laughing Brook and the Smiling Pool. Grandfather Frog and Spotty the Turtle, who are such very,

very slow travelers, had decided that the Big River was too far away, and so they would stay and live in the strange pond for a while, though it wasn't nearly so nice as their dear Smiling Pool. They had gone to sleep now, each in his own secret place where he would be safe for the night.

So Jerry Muskrat sat alone and watched. The black shadows crept farther and farther across the pond and grew blacker and blacker. Jerry didn't mind this, because, as you know, his eyes are made for seeing in the dark, and he dearly loves the night. Jerry had sat there a long time without moving. He was listening and watching. By and by he saw something that made him draw in his breath and anger leap into his eyes. It was a little silver line on the water and it was coming straight toward the dam where he sat. Jerry knew that it was made by someone swimming.

"Ha!" said Jerry. "Now we shall see!"

Nearer and nearer came the silver line. Then Jerry made out the head of the swimmer. Suddenly all the anger left Jerry. He didn't have room for anger; a great fear had crowded it out. The head was bigger than that of any Muskrat Jerry had ever seen. It was

[*145*]

bigger than the head of any of Billy Mink's relatives. It was the head of a stranger, a stranger so big that Jerry felt very, very small and hoped with all his might that the stranger would not see him.

Jerry held his breath as the stranger swam past and then climbed out on the dam. He looked very much like Jerry himself, only ever and ever so much bigger. And his tail! Jerry had never seen such a tail. It was very broad and flat. Suddenly the big stranger turned and looked straight at Jerry.

"Hello, Jerry Muskrat!" said he. "Don't you know me?"

Jerry was too frightened to speak.

[*146*]

*"Hello, Jerry Muskrat!" said he. "Don't you
know me?"*

"I'm your big cousin from the North; I'm Paddy the Beaver, and if you leave my dam alone, I think we'll be good friends," continued the stranger.

"I—I—I hope so," said Jerry in a very faint voice, trying to be polite, but with his teeth chattering with fear.

XXII

Jerry Loses His Fear

"Oh, tell me, you and you and you,
If it may hap you've ever heard
Of all that wond'rous is, and great,
The greatest is the spoken word?"

IT'S true. It's the truest thing
that ever was. If you don't believe it, you just go ask Jerry Muskrat. He'll tell you it's true, and
Jerry knows. You see, it's this way:
Words are more than just sounds.
Oh, my, yes! They are little mes-

[*149*]

sengers, and once they have been sent out, you can't call them back. No, Sir, you can't call them back, and sometimes that is a very sad thing, because—well, you see, these little messengers always carry something to someone else, and that something may be anger or hate or fear or an untruth, and it is these things which make most of the trouble in this world. Or that something may be love or sympathy or helpfulness or kindness, and it is these things which put an end to most of the troubles in this world.

Just take the case of Jerry Muskrat. There he sat on the new dam, which had made the strange pond in the Green Forest, shaking with fear until his teeth chattered, as he watched a stranger very, very much bigger than he climb up on the dam. Jerry was afraid, because he had seen that the stranger could swim as well as he could, and as Jerry had no secret burrows there, he knew that he couldn't get away from the stranger if he wanted to. Somehow, Jerry knew without being told that the stranger had built the dam, and you know Jerry had twice made a hole in the dam to let the water out of the strange pond into the Laughing Brook. Jerry knew right down in his heart that if he had built that dam, he would be very, very angry with anyone who tried to spoil it, and that is just what he had tried to do. So he sat with chattering teeth, too frightened to even try to run.

"I wish I had let someone else keep watch," said Jerry to himself. Then the big stranger had spoken. He had said, "Hello, Jerry Muskrat! Don't you know me?" and his voice hadn't sounded the least bit angry. Then he had told Jerry that he was his big cousin, Paddy the Beaver, and he hoped that they would be friends.

Now everything was just as it had been before—the strange pond,

the dam, Jerry himself and the big
stranger, and the black shadows of
the night—and yet somehow, everything was different, all because a
few pleasant words had been
spoken. A great fear had fallen
away from Jerry's heart, and in its
place was a great hope that after
all there wasn't to be any trouble.
So he replied to Paddy the Beaver
as politely as he knew how. Paddy
was just as polite, and the first
thing Jerry knew, instead of being
enemies, as Jerry had all along
made up his mind would be the
case when he found the builder of
the dam, here they were becoming
the best of friends, all because

Paddy the Beaver had said the right thing in the right way.

"But you haven't told me yet what you made those holes in my dam for, Cousin Jerry," said Paddy the Beaver finally.

Jerry didn't know just what to say. He was so pleased with his big new cousin that he didn't want to hurt his feelings by telling him that he didn't think that dam had any business to be across the Laughing Brook, and at the same time he wanted Paddy to know how he had spoiled the Laughing Brook and the Smiling Pool. At last he made up his mind to tell the whole story.

XXIII

Paddy the Beaver Does a Kind Deed

PADDY THE BEAVER listened to all that his small cousin, Jerry Muskrat, had to tell him about the trouble which Paddy's dam had caused in the Laughing Brook and the Smiling Pool.

"You see, we who live in the Smiling Pool love it dearly, and we don't want to have to leave it,

There was a twinkle in the eyes of Paddy the Beaver

but if the water cannot run down the Laughing Brook, there can be no Smiling Pool, and so we will have to move off to the Big River," concluded Jerry Muskrat. "That is why I tried to spoil your dam."

There was twinkle in the eyes of Paddy the Beaver as he replied:

"Well, now that you have found out that you can't do that, because I am bigger than you and can stop you, what are you going to do about it?"

"I don't know," said Jerry Muskrat sadly. "I don't see what we can do about it. Of course you are big and strong and can do just as you please, but it doesn't seem right that we who have lived here so long should have to move and go away from all that we love so just because you, a stranger, happen to want to live here. I tell you what!" Jerry's eyes sparkled as a brand-new thought came to him. "Couldn't you come down and live in the Smiling Pool with us? I'm sure there is room enough."

Paddy the Beaver shook his head. "No," said he, and Jerry's heart sank. "No, I can't do that because down there, there isn't any of the kind of food I eat. Besides, I wouldn't feel at all safe in the Smiling Pool. You see, I always live in the woods. No, I couldn't possibly

come down to live in the Smiling
Pool. But I'm truly sorry that I
have made you so much worry,
Cousin Jerry, and I'm going to
prove it to you. Now you sit right
here until I come back."

Before Jerry realized what he
was going to do, Paddy the Beaver
dived into the pond, and as he
disappeared, his broad tail hit the
water such a slap that it made
Jerry jump. Then there began a
great disturbance down under the
water. In a few minutes up bobbed
a stick, and then another and another, and the water grew so muddy
that Jerry couldn't see what was
going on. Paddy was gone a long

time. Jerry wondered how he could stay under water so long without air. All the time Paddy was just fooling him. He would come up to the surface, stick his nose out, nothing more, fill his lungs with fresh air, and go down again.

Suddenly Jerry Muskrat heard a sound that made him prick up his funny little short ears and whirl about so that he could look over the other side of the dam into the Laughing Brook. What do you think that sound was? Why, it was the sound of rushing water, the sweetest sound Jerry had listened to for a long time. There was a

great hole in the dam, and already
the brook was beginning to laugh
as the water rushed down it.

"How do you like that, Cousin
Jerry?" said a voice right in his ear.
Paddy the Beaver had climbed up
beside him, and his eyes were
twinkling.

"It—it's splendid!" cried Jerry.
"But—but you've spoiled your
dam!"

"Oh, that's all right," replied
Paddy. "I didn't really want it now,
anyway. I don't usually build dams
at this time of year, and I built
this one just for fun because it
seemed such a nice place to build
one. You see, I was traveling

through here, and it seemed such a nice place that I thought I would stay awhile. I didn't know anything about the Smiling Pool, you know. Now, I guess I'll have to move on and find a place where I can make a pond in the fall that will not trouble other people. You see, I don't like to be troubled myself, and so I don't want to trouble other people. This Green Forest is a very nice place."

"The very nicest place in all the world excepting the Green Meadows and the Smiling Pool!" replied Jerry promptly. "Won't you stay, Cousin Paddy? I'm sure we would all like to have you."

"Of course we would," said a gruff voice right beside them. It was Grandfather Frog.

Paddy the Beaver looked thoughtful. "Perhaps I will," said he, "if I can find some good hiding places in the Laughing Brook."

XXIV

A Merry Home-going

"The Laughing Brook is merry
And so am I," cried Jerry.
Grandfather Frog said he was, too,
And Spotty was, the others knew.

THE trees stood with wet feet
where just a little while before had been the strange pond
in the Green Forest, the pond made
by the dam of Paddy the Beaver.
In the dam was a great hole
made by Paddy himself. Through
the Green Forest rang the laughter

of the Laughing Brook, for once more the water ran deep between its banks. And in the hearts of Grandfather Frog and Jerry Muskrat and Spotty the Turtle was laughter also, for now the Smiling Pool would smile once more, and they could go home in peace and happiness. And there was one more who laughed. Who was it? Why, Paddy the Beaver, to be sure, and his was the best laugh of all, for it was because he had brought happiness to others.

"You beat me up here to the dam, but you won't beat me back to the Smiling Pool," cried Jerry Muskrat to Spotty the Turtle.

Spotty laughed good-naturedly. "You'd better not stop to eat or play or sleep on the way," said he, "for I shall keep right on going all the time. I've found that is the only way to get anywhere."

"Let us all go down together," said Grandfather Frog. "We can help each other over the bad places."

Jerry Muskrat laughed until he had to hold his sides at the very thought of Grandfather Frog or Spotty the Turtle being able to help him, but he is very good-natured, and so he agreed that they should all go down together. Paddy the Beaver said that he would go,

*"You'd better not stop to eat or play," said Spotty
the Turtle*

too, so off the four started, Jerry Muskrat and Paddy the Beaver swimming side by side, and behind them Grandfather Frog and Spotty the Turtle.

Now Spotty the Turtle is a very slow traveler on land, but in the water Spotty is not so slow. In fact, it was not long before Grandfather Frog found that he was the one who could not keep up. You see, while he is a great diver and can swim fast for a short distance, he is soon tired out. Pretty soon he was puffing and blowing and dropping farther and farther behind. By and by Spotty the Turtle looked back. There was Grandfather Frog just

tumbling headfirst over a little waterfall. He came up choking and
gasping and kicking his long legs
very feebly. Spotty climbed out on
a rock and waited. He helped
Grandfather Frog out beside him,
and when Grandfather Frog had
once more gotten his breath, what
do you think Spotty did? Why, he
took Grandfather Frog right on his
back and started on again.

Now Jerry Muskrat and Paddy
the Beaver, being great swimmers,
were soon out of sight. All at once
Jerry remembered that they had
agreed to go back together, and
down in his heart he felt a little bit
mean when he looked for Grand-

father Frog and Spotty the Turtle
and could see nothing of them. So
he and Paddy sat down to wait.
After what seemed a long time, they
saw something queer bobbing along
in the water.

"It's Grandfather Frog," cried
Paddy the Beaver.

"No, it's Spotty the Turtle," said
Jerry Muskrat.

"It's both," replied Paddy, beginning to laugh.

Just then Spotty tumbled over
another waterfall which he hadn't
seen, and of course Grandfather
Frog went with him and lost his
hold on Spotty's back.

"I have an idea!" cried Paddy.

"What is it?" asked Jerry.

"Why, Grandfather Frog can ride on my flat tail," replied Paddy, "and then we'll go slow enough for Spotty to keep up with us."

And so it was that just as the first moonbeams kissed the Smiling Pool, out of the Laughing Brook swam the merriest party that ever was seen.

"Chugarum!" said Grandfather Frog. "It is good to be home, but I think I would travel often, if I could have the tail of Paddy the Beaver for a boat."

XXV

Paddy the Beaver Decides To Stay

"The fair Green Meadows spreading wide,
The Smiling Pool and Laughing Brook—
They fill our hearts with joy and pride;
We love their every hidden nook."

SO SAID Jerry Muskrat, as he climbed up on the Big Rock in the middle of the Smiling Pool, with Paddy the Beaver beside him, and watched the dear Smiling Pool dimpling and smiling in the moonlight, as he had so often seen it before the great trouble had come.

"Chugarum!" said Grandfather Frog in his great deep voice from the bulrushes. "One never knows how great their blessings are until they have been lost and found again."

The bulrushes nodded, as if they too were thinking of this. You see, their feet were once more in the cool water. Paddy the Beaver seemed to understand just how everyone felt, and he smiled to himself as he saw how happy these new friends of his were.

"It surely is a very nice place here, and I don't wonder that you couldn't bear to leave it," said he. "I'm sorry that I made you all that trouble and worry, but you see, I didn't know."

"Oh, that's all right," replied Jerry Muskrat, who was now very proud of his big cousin. "I hope that now you see how nice it is, you will stay and make your home here."

Paddy the Beaver looked back at the great black shadow which he knew was the Green Forest. Way over in the middle of it he heard the hunting call of Hooty the Owl. Then he looked out over the Green Meadows, and from way over on the far side of them sounded the bark of Reddy Fox, and it was answered by the deep voice of Bowser the Hound up in Farmer Brown's dooryard. For some reason that last sound made Paddy the Beaver shiver a little, just as the voice of Hooty the Owl made the smaller people of the Green Forest and the Green Meadows shiver when they heard it. Paddy wasn't afraid of Hooty or of Reddy Fox, but Bowser's great voice was new to him, and somehow the very sound of it made him afraid. You see, the Green Meadows were so strange and open that he didn't feel at all at home, for he dearly loves the deepest part of the Green Forest.

"No," said Paddy the Beaver, "I can't possibly live here in the Smiling Pool. It is a very nice pool, but it wouldn't do at all for me, Cousin Jerry. I wouldn't feel safe here a minute. Besides, there is nothing to eat here."

"Oh, yes, there is," Jerry Muskrat interrupted. "There are lily roots and the nicest fresh-water clams and—"

"But there are no trees," said Paddy the Beaver, "and you know I have to have trees."

Jerry stared at Paddy as if he didn't understand. "Do—do you eat trees?" he asked finally.

Paddy laughed. "Just the bark,"

[176]

said he, "and I have to have a great deal of it."

Jerry looked as disappointed as he felt. "Of course you can't stay then," said he, "and—and I had thought that we would have such good times together."

Paddy's eyes twinkled. "Perhaps we may yet," said he. "You see, I have about made up my mind that I will stay awhile along the Laughing Brook in the Green Forest, and you can come to see me there. On our way down I saw a very nice hole in the bank that I think will make me a good house for the present, and you can come up there to see me. But if I do stay, you and

Grandfather Frog and Spotty the Turtle must keep my secret. No one must know that I am there. Will you?"

"Of course we will!" cried Jerry Muskrat and Grandfather Frog and Spotty the Turtle together.

"Then I'll stay," said Paddy the Beaver, diving into the Smiling Pool with a great splash.

And so one of Jerry Muskrat's greatest adventures ended in the finding of his biggest cousin, Paddy the Beaver. Now Jerry has a lot of cousins, and one of them lives on the Green Meadows not far from the Smiling Pool. His name is Danny Meadow Mouse, and Danny is forever having adventures too. He has them every day. In the next book you will be told about some of these, if you care to read about them.